Black Beauty

Introduction

Anna Sewell was born in 1820 in Great Yarmouth, England. She rode horses on her uncle's farm in Norfolk from a very early age; but she was often ill and had to stay in bed. She had the idea for this story when she was fifty years old, and so ill that her mother had to write it down.

Today, we ride horses mainly for pleasure. But in the nineteenth century, they were used to pull carriages or cabs, and for riders on business. Their health and happiness depended entirely on their owners and their grooms.

Anna Sewell was always shocked by the cruelty that men showed to horses at work. She wrote this story to draw attention to their poor working conditions in Victorian England. The full title page of the book was: *Black Beauty, his grooms and companions; the autobiography of a horse, translated from the original equine, by Anna Sewell.* Anna Sewell pretended that she had translated a horse's own story so that she could write from the horse's point of view. The reader *feels* what it is like to be dependent on a groom or owner.

Black Beauty was published in 1877, only a year before Anna Sewell's death. She did not live long enough to see how successful it became. Her book has been translated into many languages and has been made into a film.

CHAPTER ONE

When I was young

It was a day in early spring, when I still lived with my mother in Farmer Grey's meadow, that I first realised that life was cruel. A light mist still hung over the fields after the night frost. In the distance, I could hear the sound of dogs barking.

"Here come the hounds," said one of my friends.

We all ran to the top of the field and looked over the hedge.

"They have found a hare," explained my mother, "and if they come this way, we shall see the hunt."

Soon I could see young dogs trampling through the wheat in the next field, followed by men on horseback. The dogs did not bark, or howl, or whine, but they yelped. Suddenly, they stopped and ran round and round, their noses to the ground.

Just then, a hare ran by, wild with terror. The dogs leapt over the stream and chased it. We heard one shriek, then that was the end of her. The huntsmen rode up, held up the dead hare and seemed very pleased with themselves.

I was shocked.

A few minutes later, I heard a noise coming from the steep bank leading down to the stream. I turned round to look. A horse lay groaning on the grass, and a boy lay still beside him.

"One of the riders has fallen," said my mother, "his neck is broken."

"That serves him right," said one of the young horses.

I agreed with him, but I didn't say anything.

"Oh, no," said my mother gently, "you mustn't say that."

Now my owner was lifting up the rider, a young boy, whose arms and head hung down. Everybody looked serious. Even the dogs were quiet.

"Carry him to my house!" ordered my master, "and

fetch the doctor. Somebody go to Squire Gordon's house and tell him that his son is hurt."

We only remembered the boy's horse when the horse doctor arrived and examined him.

"Broken leg!" he said.

He took out his gun and shot the poor animal.

"I've known that horse for years," said my mother quietly, "he's called Rob Roy. He was a brave and good horse."

She sobbed loudly.

"I'll never come to this part of the field again," she wept.

Squire Gordon's son also died that day and he was buried a few days later.

"All because of one little hare," I thought.

I grew into a handsome horse. By the time I was almost four, my coat had grown fine and soft, and was bright black. I had one white foot, a white star on my forehead and a splash of white on my back.

One day, Squire Gordon came to look at me.

"When you have broken him in, he will suit me very well," he told my owner.

Do you know what
breaking in a horse means?
It means to teach a horse to
wear a saddle and reins and
to carry a person on its back,
or in a carriage behind him.

It was not too terrible. The thing I hated most was the iron shoes I had to wear. They were stiff and heavy. But I soon got used to them.

Soon, it was time to leave my mother and go to Squire Gordon's estate.

"Remember," she said, "the better you behave, the better you will be treated."

She looked at me for a moment.

"There are many kinds of men," she went on, "good, bad, foolish, ignorant, careless and, worst of all, cruel ones who should never be allowed to own a horse. I hope you will always have a good master."

Her face was sad now.

"A horse never knows who will buy him. But I still say, do your best wherever it is, and keep up your good name."

With those last words, she left me. And I went to begin my new life at Birtwick Park.

CHAPTER TWO
A stormy day

I was nervous when my new master came to ride me for the first time. I tried to do exactly what he wanted me to do. Squire Gordon was a good rider, and very thoughtful towards me. He took me to meet his wife.

"He is a pleasant creature," the Squire told her. "What shall we call him?"

"Would you like Ebony?" she asked. "He is as black as ebony wood."

"No, not Ebony," said her husband.

"Blackbird?" she suggested, "like your uncle's old horse?"

"No," he replied, "he is far more handsome than old Blackbird ever was."

"Yes," agreed his wife, "he really is quite a beauty. He has such a sweet-tempered face, and such intelligent eyes. Why don't we call him Black Beauty?"

"Black Beauty it is!" laughed the Squire.

"I would have called him Rob Roy," said James, the stable-boy, to his friend. "I've never seen two horses more alike."

"That's because they had the same mother," replied his friend.

I felt sad. Poor Rob Roy who was killed at the hunt had been my brother!

I soon made friends with Merrylegs and Ginger, the other horses in my stable, and we spent many happy times talking under the apple trees in the orchard. I liked Merrylegs, a small, plump pony who belonged to the Squire's children; but at first, I was a little afraid of Ginger, a tall chestnut mare, because she was so bad-tempered. Then I learned later that she had been badly treated in the past. We soon became good friends. We were both good for riding and for driving because we both had some racing blood in us. And we were both about the right height – fifteen and a half hands high.

I was very happy in my new home. I had a light, airy stable and plenty of good food. What more could I want? Well, I wanted my freedom! For the first three and a half years of my life, I had run and jumped in the fresh air, in green fields. But now, week after week, month after month (and probably year after year!), I had to stand up in my stable. I only went outside when somebody needed me. I was young and I longed to gallop over the fields with my tail blowing in the wind.

John, the coachman, knew this. Sometimes, he used to ride me through the village and into the hills for a while. He knew how to calm my high spirits. Other horses are not so lucky. Their masters beat them to quieten them.

But one stormy autumn day, I had more exercise than I wanted.

My master had to make a long business journey. John harnessed me to a small light carriage, then sat on top with the master. The wind was blowing hard and there had been a lot of rain during the night. Soon, we came to a small wooden bridge. I looked down in surprise. The river was very high, and still rising.

My master went into the town on business and we set off for home later than usual. The wind shrieked in the trees and the branches swayed like twigs.

"I've never been out in such bad weather," John said.

"I wish we were well out of this wood," replied the master.

Suddenly, there was a groan, and a crack and a splitting sound. An oak tree fell right across the road in front of us. I was very frightened and I stopped, trembling. But I am proud to say that I did not turn around or start to run.

"Well, sir," said John, "we can't drive over that tree nor round it. We shall have to go back to the crossroads. It will be at least six miles before we get round to the wooden bridge again. But the horse is fresh."

It was almost dark by the time we got back to the bridge. We could see the water over the middle of it. I was going fast, but the moment my feet touched the first part of the bridge, I felt that something was wrong.

"Go on, Beauty," said my master. He whipped me gently at first, then hard.

I refused to move.

"Come on, Beauty, what's the matter?" asked John.

I wanted to tell him that the bridge was dangerous; but of course, I couldn't. Just then, the man at the bridge toll-gate, on the other side of the river, saw us and came out.

"Stop! Stop!" he shouted above the wind. "The bridge is broken in the middle. The water has swept some of it away."

"Thank God!" said my master.

"You Beauty!" said John as he gently turned me round.

We travelled in silence for a while. Then I heard my master's voice.

"We would have all been carried away by the water," he said, "we would have all been drowned. God has given animals a special knowledge. They act rather than think. This is how they often save men's lives."

What a wonderful supper John gave me when we arrived home – a good bran mash, some crushed beans with my oats and a thick bed of straw. I sank into it gratefully. I had never been so tired.

I did not know then that soon that I would be in even greater danger.

CHAPTER THREE
The fire!

My master and mistress decided to visit to some friends who lived about forty-six miles from our home. James was to drive them. On the way, we spent the night at a hotel in the market place of a small town. One of the grooms who worked there led me and Ginger into the stables.

Another groom came in later, with another traveller's horse. This groom was younger and smoked a pipe.

"I say," the old groom said to him, "just run up the ladder into the hay loft and let some hay down, will you? But put down your pipe first."

"All right," said the boy, and he climbed through the trap door into the loft.

Soon afterwards, the men locked the stable door and left. During the night, I suddenly woke up. I felt very uncomfortable. What was wrong? The air around me was thick and smoky. I could hear Ginger coughing. The other horses were restless. Then I realised. It was smoke!

I listened carefully. Above me, in the hay loft, I could hear a soft rushing noise, then a crackling sound. I trembled all over. The other horses were awake by now. They were beginning to rear on their hind legs.

At that moment, the stable door burst open. One of the grooms came in with a lantern and began to untie the horses nearest to the door.

"Come on! Come on!" he shouted.

The horses could hear the fear in his voice and they would not go with him. Then he tried to pull me; but I refused to move too.

"I know it's silly," I thought, "but I don't trust him."

Fresh air came through the open door. I could breathe more easily. But a red light still flickered all around us.

"Fire! Fire!" shouted somebody outside.

Then I heard James's voice, quiet and cheery as usual.

"Come on, my beauties, it's time for us to be off. Wake up!" he called out.

He came over to me and tied his scarf over my eyes. He patted me gently, then led me out of the stable. In the yard, he took off the scarf and went back for another horse. I was so nervous that I started to whinny loudly.

I stood looking at the stable door. Thick smoke poured from it and flashes of red lit up the darkness. I heard a loud crash inside the stable. What had happened to Ginger? The next moment, I neighed happily. James was walking out of the smoke, leading Ginger. They were both coughing violently.

"My brave lad," said the master to James, "are you hurt?"

James shook his head. Ginger staggered over to me.

"Thank goodness you made that awful noise," she gasped. "I only had the courage to move because I heard you outside."

The noise from the stable was awful. The two horses still inside shrieked as they burned to death. It was a terrible night – and all because that boy had gone up into the hay loft smoking his pipe.

CHAPTER FOUR

Night ride

Soon after the fire, James got ready to leave us. He was going to work as a groom for the master's brother-in-law.

"I wonder who is coming in my place," he said one night to John.

"Little Joe Green," John replied.

"Little Joe Green!" cried James. "Why, he's a child!"

"He is fourteen and a half," said John, "and he is quick and willing to learn. I shall try him for six weeks."

"Six weeks!" said James, "it will be six months before he can be any use."

I often thought of his words in the weeks that followed.

A few days after James had left, I was fast asleep one night, when the stable bell began to ring loudly. John ran in.

"Wake up, Beauty, you must run as fast as you can," he said, slipping on my saddle and bridle.

I stood up, half-asleep. Was I dreaming? No! John led me to the front door of the Hall where the master stood with a lamp in his hand.

"Now, John," he said seriously, "ride for your life..."

He stopped. I pricked up my ears. Something was wrong.

"...for your mistress's life," he continued. "Give this note to Doctor White."

"Yes, sir," said John.

We galloped through the Park, through the village and down the hill to the riverside.

"Now, Beauty, do your best," shouted John.

I did. I galloped as fast as I could put my feet on the ground. When we came to the bridge, John pulled me up.

"Well done, Beauty! Good old fellow," he said.

Soon I was off again, as fast as before. The air was frosty. The moon was bright. On and on I ran, through the wood, uphill, then downhill, eight miles in all. I clattered into the town as the church clock struck three o' clock.

John knocked on Dr. White's door with a noise like thunder. At last a bedroom window opened.

"What do you want?" shouted Dr. White.

"Mrs. Gordon is very ill, sir. Master wants you to go at once. He thinks she will die if you cannot get there," said John. "Here is a note."

"Wait," said Dr. White, "I will come."

He hurried down to us.

"My own horse has been out all day,"

he said, "can I take yours?"

I was very hot and tired by this time. I needed a rest.

To my alarm, I saw that the doctor was carrying a riding whip.

"You will not need that, sir," said John. "Black Beauty will run until he drops."

I felt very proud when I heard his words.

We set off. I will not say much about our ride back. Only that the doctor was a heavy man, and he was a poor rider. I did my best, as my mother had always taught me. When I finally got to my stable that night, my legs were shaking under me. I panted heavily and the sweat poured from me. Steam began to rise from my back.

Little Joe Green did his best, too. He rubbed my legs and chest. He gave me a bucket of water to drink and a bed of hay. But he didn't put my warm cloth on me because I was so hot. Soon, I began to shiver with cold.

"I wish John was here," I groaned, "but he has eight miles to walk! He wouldn't have forgotten my warm cloth."

I couldn't sleep. My body ached too much. I moaned and groaned. Much later, when I heard the stable door open, I looked up. It was John! I gave another moan. John came straight over to me with three warm cloths and hot water for me to drink.

As I went to sleep, I heard him talking to himself.

"Stupid boy! Stupid boy!" he muttered. "No cloth put on, and I dare say the water was cold too. Boys are no good."

By the morning, I was very ill.

CHAPTER FIVE

A new home

My lungs hurt a great deal and I could not breathe very easily. John nursed me day and night. One day, my master came to see me.

"My poor Beauty," he said, "my good horse, you saved your mistress's life."

I do not know how long I was ill. I had a high fever and the slightest noise seemed very loud. Merrylegs and Ginger were moved to the end of the stable. John gave me some medicine one night, helped by Tom Green. I listened to their chatter.

"I wish you would say a kind word to my lad," said Tom, "he's broken-hearted. He can't eat, he can't smile. He says he knows it's his fault. He said he did his best. Just one kind word. Joe's not a bad boy."

"I know that, Tom," John said at last, "but that horse is my pride and joy. And my master and mistress's favourite. I will try to say a good word tomorrow – that is, I mean, if Beauty is better."

"Thank you, John," said Tom, "I'm glad you see it was only ignorance."

John's voice was so loud and angry that it made me jump.

"*Only* ignorance! Only *ignorance*!" he shouted. "How can you talk about *only* ignorance? Don't you know it's the worst thing in the world next to wickedness?"

His voice faded away as I slept properly for the first time. And when I woke up, I *was* much better. I often thought of John's words when I had to go out into the cruel world that lay outside Birtwick Park.

It was John who brought the bad news to the stable.

"The mistress is ill again," he told Joe, "the doctor has said she and the master must live in a warm country."

Joe hardly ever whistled after that. John was always silent and sad.

"I have sold Ginger and Black Beauty to a friend of mine at Earshall Park," the master told John. "And Merrylegs will go to the Vicar. Joe can look after him there. What can I do for you, John?"

"Nothing, thank you, sir," he replied. "I've had some good job offers, but I want to take my time and think about it."

On the night before the family left, the master came to say goodbye. He patted us for the last time. He was very sad. I knew that by his voice. I believe we horses can tell more by the voice than many men can. I was sad too. The longer I had lived at Birtwick Park, the happier and prouder I had become.

The next day, John rode us to Earshall Park. Then he

left soon afterwards to catch his train. I held my face close to him. That was all I could do to say good-bye. I have never seen him since.

My new master seemed pleased with us. In the afternoon, his groom, York, harnessed us to the ladyship's carriage. I didn't like my new rein at all. It was short and tight, to keep our heads high in the air. I couldn't put my head down. Her ladyship was not happy with the way we looked and shouted for the groom.

"York!" she called. "You must put these horses' heads higher. They are not fit to be seen."

"I beg your pardon, my lady," said York, "but these horses have not been reined up for three years. My lord has told me to bring their heads up slowly."

"Do it now!" she replied.

As we rode up the hill, I understood why horses hated these reins so much. I wanted to put my head forward as I climbed. Now I had to pull the carriage uphill, with my head held high. It took all the spirit out of me. And it hurt my back and legs. Every day, the rein was tightened a little more. I began to dread my harness.

One day, her ladyship was more angry than usual.

"Tighten the reins again," she told York.

He tightened mine first, so much that I could hardly bear it. Then he went over to Ginger. She reared and knocked off his hat, then started to kick. After a long struggle, York led her back to the stable. Our master was angry when he heard.

"You should not have given in to her ladyship," he told York.

I nodded in agreement.

"York should stand up for his horses," I muttered to Ginger.

Ginger was never put in the carriage again. And later, she went to work for one of the master's sons. Now I had a new carriage partner called Max.

"You never complain about the short rein," I said to him. "How can you bear it?"

"Well," he said, "I bear it because I must. But it is shortening my life, and it will shorten yours."

"Do our masters know how bad it is for us?" I asked him.

"I don't know," said Max, "but the horse doctors do."

I cannot describe how much I suffered during the next four months. The mouth rein hurt my tongue and jaw, and I often frothed at the mouth. Some people thought this was what horses did. However, it is as bad for a horse to froth at the mouth as it is for a man.

Soon, I was worn out and depressed. And far worse, nobody seemed to care. But soon I suffered much greater pain and it changed my life for ever.

CHAPTER SIX
Ruined

For a few weeks, my life became easier. The Earl took his wife to London for a short stay. Sometimes, his daughter, Lady Anne, rode me. I enjoyed my rides with her in the clear, cold air.

A man called Reuben Smith was left in charge of the stables. He was gentle and clever and knew a great deal about horses. Everybody liked him, especially the horses. But he had one great fault - a love of drink, and that caused me more pain than my short reins.

It was a day in early April, a month before the family was to return from London. Smith had driven me to town. He left me at the blacksmith's and went to meet his friends. I waited. Six o'clock, seven o'clock, eight o' clock. Where was he? He fetched me at nine o'clock, shouting and bellowing.

Once outside the town, Smith began to whip me, although I was running at top speed. It was very dark. The road had just been mended and loose stones flew into my face. One of my shoes came loose. Smith beat me harder. The sharp stones began to split my shoeless hoof.

I fell onto my knees, throwing Smith to the ground. He groaned and I could have groaned too; but horses are used to bearing their pain in silence. I managed to get to my feet but my knees were very painful.

The moon had risen now. The air was calm and smelled sweet, and a brown owl flitted over the hedge. I remembered the summer nights, when I was young, when I used to lie next to my mother in the fields. I waited and listened for the noise of a horse or carriage.

It was almost midnight when I heard the sound of horse's hooves. I recognised Ginger's step! I neighed loudly, and she neighed back. The men with her went over to Reuben.

"He's dead!" they said. "Who would have thought the black horse would have done such a thing?"

I could not walk without falling again.

"Poor fellow!" said Robert, one of the grooms. "His hoof is cut to pieces. No wonder he fell."

He sighed.

"Reuben has been up to his old tricks again. Just think of him riding a horse over these stones without a shoe!"

I shall never forget that walk home. Robert led me slowly. I limped and hobbled in great pain. I healed in time, but I never lost the scars. It was the beginning of the end for me. When the master came home in May, he examined me angrily.

"I do not mind about the money," he said, "but I promised my old friend I would give his horse a good home."

He looked at me again.

"It is a great pity, but this black one must be sold. I cannot have knees like this in my stables."

Just a week later, Robert came to take me to the railway station. I did not have time to say good-bye to Ginger. She trotted by the side of the hedge as I walked on the road, and neighed to me as long as she could hear the sound of my feet.

Ginger was right. It is a hard life.

I travelled by train to my new master, a man who hired out horses and carriages. I was popular because I was good-tempered. Unfortunately, this meant that I was ridden by all sorts of people, and many of them didn't know how to treat a horse. Some of them were just lazy. Then they let the horses get into bad habits, which means that it is difficult for the next driver. I remember what Squire Gordon used to say,

"It's just as cruel to spoil a horse as it is to spoil a child. They both have to suffer for it later on."

I remember one really cruel and careless driver. I was pulling a small carriage for him, a lady and two children. He whipped me as we set off and paid no attention to the loose stones on the road. Soon, I got a stone in one of my front feet. I began to limp and stumble with the pain.

"Why, they have sent us a lame horse!" called the

driver at last. "What a shame!"

He whipped me again.

"It's no use turning lame and lazy with me," he shouted, "not when there's a journey to do."

Just then, a farmer rode by. He raised his hat politely.

"I beg your pardon, sir," he said, "but I think there is something the matter with your horse. Let me look. These loose stones are dangerous for a horse."

That kind farmer took out the stone for me, and I managed the rest of the journey.

I was happy to be sold after a short time to a Mr. Barry who wanted a safe, pleasant horse for riding. Then I was at the mercy of my groom! My master knew very little about horses, but he treated me well. He ordered the best hay with plenty of oats, crushed beans, and bran and rye grass.

But I was starving, all because of my groom, Filcher. For about two months, he gave me very little food. He used to come in every morning at about six o' clock with his young son who filled a little basket with *my* oats! I began to lose my strength.

One day, my master went riding with a friend.

"It seems to me," said the friend, "that your horse does not look as well as when you first had him. Has he been well?"

"My groom tells me that horses are always dull in the autumn," said my master.

"Nonsense!" said his friend, "this is only August!"

Soon after this conversation, Filcher was sent to prison for stealing and I had a new groom called Alfred Smirk. What would he be like? Unfortunately, it did not take me long to find out that he was no better.

In front of my master, he was always very kind, patting and stroking and brushing me. I looked smart, but he never cleaned me properly, or my stable. He never took all the dirty straw away. Soon, a strong smell rose from the bottom layer of straw. It stung my eyes and put me off my food. Then my feet became unhealthy and tender from standing too long in the damp. I began to stumble. These grooms did more than damage my health. They caused my master to give me up altogether.

"Since I cannot trust my grooms, I shall hire a horse when I need one," he said angrily.

And that was how I came to be sold at a horse fair.

CHAPTER SEVEN
Life as a cab horse

I was shocked by some of the horses I saw when I arrived at the fair. Poor things, they were sadly broken down by their hard work – their knees bent, ribs showing, and old sores on their backs and hips. But who knows, I might be in the same state one day!

All day long, people came to look at me; but they never wanted to pay the full price. The gentlemen always turned away from me when they saw my broken knees. There was one man that I liked. He had grey eyes with a kind, cheery look in them. He handled me well, and I hoped that he would buy me.

He *did* buy me. He rode me all the way home – to London. The gas lamps were lit in the streets by the time we arrived. I had never seen so many streets. Soon we turned up one of the side streets with poor-looking houses on one side, and stables on the other.

My owner whistled outside one of the doors. A woman and two children ran out.

"Now then, Harry, my boy, open the gates," shouted my owner.

He led me into a small stable yard.

"Is he gentle, father?" asked the girl.

"Yes, Dolly, as gentle as your own kitten. Come and pat him. We'll call him Jack."

A little hand patted my shoulders. How good it felt!

My new master's name was Jeremiah Barker, but everyone called him Jerry. I have never seen such a happy family before, or since. Jerry had his own cab, and one other horse called Captain, an old army horse, who must have been a fine horse in his day.

My first week as a cab horse was very hard. The noise, the hurry, the crowds of horses, carts and carriages made me nervous and anxious. But I soon found that I could trust my driver. He quickly found out that I was willing to work, and to do my best. He *never* whipped me. In a short time, we understood each other as well as a horse and a man can.

My new master became cross when people asked him to drive hard if they were late because of their laziness. But he would always hurry if there was a good reason. I remember one morning when we were waiting at the cab stand for passengers. A young man slipped on a piece of orange peel right in front of us. Jerry helped him to his feet.

"Thank you," said the young man. "Now can you please take me to the South-Eastern Railway? I must catch the twelve o' clock train. I will gladly pay you extra."

"I'll do my very best," said Jerry cheerfully, "if you think

you are well enough, sir, for you look very pale and ill."

"I must go," said the young man.

That young man caught his train, thanks to Jerry. And he would not take a penny more for the fare.

However, my new master's strong opinions did not please everybody. One morning, a gentleman called Mr. Briggs walked into the yard.

"Good morning," he said, "I have come to make some arrangements with you. Mrs. Briggs would like you to take her to church on Sunday mornings."

Jerry did not look pleased.

"Thank you, sir," he said, "but I only have a cab licence for six days. I cannot work on a Sunday."

"You can easily alter your licence," said Mr. Briggs.

"I had a seven-day licence once," said Jerry. "The work was too hard for me and too hard for my horses."

"I understand," said the gentleman, "but we are very good customers. It would only be a short distance for the horse. You would have the rest of the day for yourself."

"I cannot give up my Sundays, sir," said Jerry. "I am stronger and healthier now that I have a day of rest. The horses do not wear so fast."

For three weeks after this conversation, Mr. and Mrs. Briggs did not use our cab. It soon became known that Jerry had lost his best customer. But they came back to us. They could not find anybody they liked better!

For a cab horse, I was very well off. My driver was my owner and he treated me well. I did not realise how lucky I was until the day I saw Ginger again.

CHAPTER EIGHT

Poor Ginger

One day, whilst our cab was waiting outside one of the parks where a band was playing, a shabby old cab came up beside us. I stared at the horse. She was an old, worn-out chestnut, with an ill-kept coat, and bones that showed through.

I had been eating hay and the wind blew some of it towards her. The poor creature put out her long thin neck and picked it up. Then she looked around for more. There was a hopeless look in her dull eyes.

"Where have I seen that horse before?" I thought.

As I was thinking, the horse stared at me.

"Black Beauty, is that you?" she whispered.

I could hardly believe my eyes! It was Ginger. How she had changed! Her arched neck was now straight and fallen in. Her fine legs were swollen, her joints out of shape. Her face, once so lively, was full of suffering. She coughed all the time and her breath was bad.

Our drivers were standing together, so I went close to her so that we might have a quiet little talk. It was a sad tale that she had to tell.

"What happened to you after I left Earshall?" I asked.

"They rested me for a year, then sold me," she answered. "I was with a very nice gentleman. But he worked me so hard that I had to rest. I have been sold several times for that reason." She sighed. "I have gone lower and lower each time."

"How have you got into this sorry state?" I asked.

"I was bought by a man who hires out cabs," she told me. "They are just using me up now. They whip me and work me. They never think of what I might be suffering. It's all the week round, with never a Sunday rest."

"You used to stand up for yourself if you were treated badly," I reminded her sadly.

"Ah, yes," she said. "I did once. But it's no use. Men are stronger than us. If they are cruel, there's nothing we can do. We just have to bear it until..."

Her eyes filled with tears.

"...until we die."

Her voice sank to a whisper.

"I wish I could drop dead at my work," she said softly.

I was upset. I touched her nose with mine to comfort her. I didn't know what to say.

"You are the only friend I ever had," she whispered.

Just then, her driver came up and, with a tug at the rein, drove her off. I was very sad indeed.

A week or two after this, a cart carrying a dead horse

passed our cab stand. In it was a chestnut horse with a long, thin neck. Its head hung over the back of the cart, its lifeless tongue dropping blood, its eyes sunk into its head. I still shudder when I think of it. I looked at the white streak down the horse's forehead.

"It *must* be Ginger," I thought.

I cried a little. Then I thought, "I'm glad. Now her suffering is over."

CHAPTER NINE
Election day

There was great excitement in London and in the whole country. There was to be an election soon. Just before the big day, Polly came rushing out of the house when we came home.

"Jerry," she said, "I've had one of those election gentleman here just now. He wants to hire your cab on election day. And he hopes that you will vote for *him*."

"Running about to the public houses to fetch half-drunken men to vote," grumbled Jerry. "It's an insult to the horses. I won't do it!"

"But you'll be voting for the gentleman, surely?" asked Polly.

"No," said Jerry firmly, "I won't. He's a rich man who doesn't know what working class men want."

He looked sternly at Polly.

"An election is a very serious thing and every man should vote how he really wants," he said.

Of course, election day brought us plenty of work. Jerry had to put on my nose-bag of oats because we had no time to stop for food. But we horses had a bad time that day! Drunken people rushed about in the streets and two people were knocked down.

"I never want to see another election," I muttered to myself.

I remember how kind my master was that day, and not just to me. He caught sight of a young woman at the side of the street. She was carrying a crying child.

"Do you know the way to St. Thomas' Hospital?" she asked Jerry.

"Well, you can't walk all that way," said Jerry, "not in these crowds, and carrying a child. It's more than three miles."

"I can do it," she said, looking around her nervously. "I wish I'd known there was an election. I've never seen such crowds."

"You might get knocked down," said Jerry. "Now just get into this cab and I'll take you."

"No, sir," said the woman, "I can't do that, thank you. I don't have enough money."

"Look," said Jerry gently, "I've got a wife and children of my own. I'll take you there for nothing."

The woman burst into tears. Jerry went to open the door for her. At the same time, two men pushed past him and got into the cab.

"This cab is already engaged by this lady!" shouted Jerry.

"*She* can wait," said one of the men. "*Our* business is important."

"I can wait," Jerry called. "You won't be going anywhere in this cab."

The men soon got out, shouting and swearing at Jerry. Then we set off for the hospital.

"Thank you! Thank you!" cried the woman as we arrived. "I could never have got here by myself."

"You're welcome," said Jerry, "and I hope the child is better soon."

Then he patted my neck as he always did when he was pleased with me. And I was pleased with him. He was the best master I had ever had.

CHAPTER TEN
Hard times

Christmas week came. There is no holiday for the cabmen and their horses. Sometimes, we have to wait for hours in the rain or frost, shivering with cold while people are dancing to the music inside.

On the evening of the New Year, Jerry had a very bad cough. We waited for two gentlemen who were playing cards until eleven o' clock. The wind blew sleet into our faces. When we left two hours later, Jerry was very ill.

Harry came to feed and clean me for the next few weeks. I missed Jerry and I was worried about him. He did slowly get better, but the doctor said that he must never go back to cab work again. One day, Dolly came into the stable. She could hardly speak for excitement.

"Oh, Harry, there was never anything so beautiful!" she laughed. "We are going to live in the country, in a house with a garden and apple trees."

"That's just the right thing," said Harry. "I'll be a groom or a gardener."

I felt very sad. I was not young now and three years of cab work had weakened me. I was sold to a baker long before Jerry was allowed out of bed, and I never said goodbye to him.

"Poor old Jack! Dear old Jack! I wish we could take you with us," wept Polly. Then she put her face close to my mane and kissed me.

I had to carry very heavy loads in my new job. And even worse, my driver Jakes always pulled the bearing rein tight. One day, I was struggling to pull the load up a steep hill. I had to stop. Jakes whipped me.

"Get on, you lazy fellow," he said.

I struggled on again. Jakes whipped me harder. My mind was as hurt as my body. Suddenly, I heard a lady's voice.

"Oh! Please do not whip your good horse any more. I am sure he is doing his best."

"He must do something more than his best, that's all I know, ma'am," said Jakes.

The lady looked at my tight bearing rein.

"The horse cannot use all his power with his head held back like that," she said. "I would be very glad if you would take it off."

"Well, well," laughed Jakes, "anything to please a lady."

He took off my rein and I walked more easily up the hill.

"You won't put that rein on again, will you?" asked the lady.

"If he went without it, ma'am, I should be a laughing stock. It is the fashion, you see."

"Is it not better," said the lady, "to start a good fashion, than to follow a bad one?"

Jake did loosen my rein after that whenever we went uphill; but his loads were just as heavy. Soon, a younger horse replaced me.

I shall never forget my new master, Nicholas Skinner. He had black eyes, a hooked nose and a mouth full of huge teeth. His voice was as harsh as a cart wheel on gravel stones. I never knew until then the real horror of a cab horse's life. I had no Sunday rest. I was hired out hour after hour. I hardly rested or ate.

I wished that I could drop dead at my work, like dear Ginger. And one day, I *nearly* got my wish.

I was taking a family and their luggage from the railway station. On the way, my feet slipped from under me. The shock of the fall took all the breath from my body. I lay perfectly still. I thought I was going to die.

"Oh! That poor horse! It is all our fault," said one of the children.

"He's dead. He'll never get up again," said somebody else.

I did not die. I staggered to my feet and went back to Skinner's stables.

"He might get well – or he might not," said Skinner. "That sort of thing don't suit my business. I work 'em as long as they go, and then sell 'em."

I was lucky this time. There was a horse sale in ten days' time. My owner let me rest until then, hoping to get a better price for me. I began to think that it would be better to live after all. At the sale, I held up my head and hoped for the best.

I noticed a man with broad shoulders and a kind, rosy face. A young boy was at his side. They came over to me. I stood there hopefully. I still had a good mane and tail.

"There's a horse, Willie, that has known better days," said the man.

"Poor old fellow," said the boy. "Do you think, Grandpapa, he was ever a carriage horse?"

"Oh yes, my boy," said his grandfather, coming closer. "Look at his nostrils and his ears, the shape of his neck and his shoulder. There's a deal of breeding about this horse."

He gave me a kind pat on the neck. The boy stroked my face.

"I am sure he would grow young on our farm, Grandpapa," he said.

"My dear boy," laughed his grandfather, "I can't make all old horses young."

"Please, Grandpapa!" begged the boy. "Although he is very thin, he is not so old."

The farmer led me out for a trot. I arched my poor thin neck, raised my tail a little and threw out my legs as